'Grib
drea...   ...an
breathed hard.

Absolutely nothing happened.

Gribble began to feel quite cross. He gave an
enormous sniff and blew as hard as he could out
of his mouth and nose at the same time.

A miserable trickle of yellow smoke came out of
the corner of his jaws and wound round his left
ear.

Gribble was very upset.'

But things go from bad to worse when Gribble
realizes that, if he can't breathe any fire, he can't
cook his breakfast! What could be wrong with
him? Perhaps his friend Cadwallader can
help . . .

DRAGON FIRE is the first in a series of
adventures about Gribble, the lovable little
dragon.

BY MYSELF books are specially selected to be suitable for beginner readers. Other BY MYSELF books available from Young Corgi Books include:

YOUR GUESS IS AS GOOD AS MINE by Bernard Ashley
MIDNIGHT PIRATE by Diana Hendry
THE TALE OF THE CROOKED CRAB by Delia Huddy
URSULA CAMPING by Sheila Lavelle
THE HAUNTING OF HEMLOCK HALL by Lance Salway
MY GANG by Catherine Sefton
THE KILLER TADPOLE by Jacqueline Wilson

DRAGON FIRE

Ann Ruffell

Illustrated by Andrew Brown

YOUNG CORGI BOOKS

For my god-daughter, Ruth

DRAGON FIRE

A YOUNG CORGI BOOK 0 552 52445X

Originally published in Great Britain in 1979 by
Hamish Hamilton Children's Books

PRINTING HISTORY
Young Corgi edition published 1987

This book is set in 18/24 pt Garamond
by Colset Private Limited, Singapore.

Young Corgi Books are published by Transworld Publishers
Ltd., 61–63 Uxbridge Road, Ealing, London W5 5SA, in
Australia by Transworld Publishers (Australia) Pty. Ltd., 15–23
Helles Avenue, Moorebank, NSW 2170, and in New Zealand
by Transworld Publishers (N.Z.) Ltd., Cnr. Moselle and
Waipareira Avenues, Henderson, Auckland.

Made and printed in Great Britain by
The Guernsey Press Co. Ltd., Guernsey, Channel Islands.

Chapter 1

Gribble was a dragon.

Like all dragons, he lived on a mountain. Most dragons prefer to live in volcanoes, because they are nice and warm. However, there are more dragons than volcanoes, so there are always a few who have to live on ordinary cold mountains.

This particular morning Gribble woke with a sore throat and a sniffly nose. He yawned, then wished he hadn't. It made his throat feel like stretched sandpaper. He wiped his nose with one of his wings.

His cave felt very, very cold. Gribble shivered, and his scales rattled all the way down his back like pennies being poured out of

a money box. It was a very odd feeling. He had never felt cold in his life before, and for a moment he wondered what was wrong.

Of course, with his stuffy nose he hadn't been breathing nice warm air into his cave. Now if only he lived in a volcano, it would be warm all the time.

He opened his mouth and breathed hard. Any other day he would have poured out enough heat to melt a glacier, one of those great rivers of ice which used to carve their way down the mountain long before Gribble lived there.

Nothing happened.

Gribble sneezed and wondered if he was dreaming. He opened his mouth again and breathed hard.

Absolutely nothing happened.

Gribble began to feel quite cross. He gave an enormous sniff and blew as hard as he could out of his mouth and nose at the same time.

A miserable trickle of yellow smoke came out of the corner of his jaws and wound round his left ear.

Gribble was very upset.

'Must be the sore throat,' he thought. 'I'd better take a pill.'

He flapped his way through to the kitchen, which was in a second cave farther inside the mountain: so far inside that the

heat could not get out very quickly. It felt just like a volcano on baking days. Gribble wished he could live in a real volcano, but you had to be very old before you could get one of them.

Today the kitchen was not warm at all. Last night's heat had disappeared right into the middle of the mountain. Gribble breathed on his breakfast mutton. Usually this made the kitchen light up in a friendly way, but today the cave filled with horrible, smelly smoke.

Gribble coughed, and flapped at it with his leathery wings. The smoke chased round the kitchen, playing hide and seek with him, but did not go out. Gribble coughed even more, and tried to remember where he had put the pills. At last he saw them: a large jar marked 'Dragon Pills' at the back of the highest shelf.

Gribble took three, the proper dose for his age, which was a hundred and fifty years, and

washed them down with a glass of paraffin. He sat down in front of the mutton and waited for the pills to take effect.

He was pretty hungry and the mutton looked very good. He breathed and bit, all in one movement, as he usually did. The fire from his mouth and nostrils would cook his breakfast, making it crisp and crunchy outside and pink and juicy inside.

It was quite awful! The meat was not cooked at all and the outside had turned a nasty yellow from the smoke.

Gribble was getting really cross.

'Even, the smallest, stupidest dragon,' he muttered, trying to blow the smoke away and making things ten times worse, 'can puff a fireball from the cradle!'

The mutton was ruined, covered in stinking paraffin fumes.

The dragon pills weren't going to work, Gribble thought. And even if they did now, his breakfast was uneatable.

Chapter 2

He sniffed and coughed, then suddenly felt more cheerful.

There was Cadwallader, his next-door neighbour.

He was not a particular friend of Cadwallader. Dragons are

not very friendly creatures. But Cadwallader might possibly have something left over which he could have for breakfast. Perhaps a spare leg of mutton.

He flew across the valley to where Cadwallader had his cave.

'Are you there, Cadwallader?'
he shouted.

'No,' said a gritty voice. 'Why? What's the matter? You can't be visiting at breakfast time.'

'I need help,' said Gribble anxiously, sniffing a wonderful smell amongst the smoke and steam.

'Just a moment,' said Cadwallader. 'Can you come back after breakfast?'

'Not after mine,' said Gribble. 'I haven't anything to eat for breakfast.'

Cadwallader popped his head out of the cave and looked suspiciously at Gribble.

'I hope you haven't come to eat any of mine,' he said severely.

'Oh, no,' said Gribble hastily. His mouth was watering so much that sooty drops fell from the corner of his mouth and sizzled on the hot ground.

'What I mean is,' he went on, 'I have half a sheep to eat, but I can't cook it.'

He opened his mouth and blew to show what he meant.

Cadwallader backed away into

his cave, coughing.

'There's something wrong with you, Gribble,' he said from the safety of his kitchen. 'You'd better see a doctor.'

'I will,' said Gribble. But he was very hungry and could not stop himself from asking, 'Can you spare any breakfast first?'

'Sorry, old chap,' said Cadwallader. 'Only a tiny bit left. Not worth it. But bring yours along any time and I'll cook it for you.'

Gribble thought of his mutton, completely spoiled by yellow smoke and paraffin.

'Don't bother, I'll manage,' he said politely, but added 'Mean thing,' as he flew back to his own cave.

The nearest dragon doctor lived hundreds of miles away near a volcano called Etna. He would have to cross the Channel, fly down through France, and go very high over the Alps into Italy.

Chapter 3

It was nearly lunch time when Gribble arrived, past the toe of Italy and on to the island where the volcano called Etna was. The weather had grown hotter and hotter as he travelled farther south. Gribble became hotter and hotter too. He was sure he had a temperature.

Etna puffed out smoke in a lazy way. Gribble could see the glow of red-hot rock as he flew over the top of the mountain. It ought to have made him feel warm and comfortable, but he

was so hot and ill that the volcano made him feel worse.

The dragon doctor lived in a house just below Etna. A very old dragon lived in the volcano itself, but he was so ancient that he never came out of his cave.

The dragon doctor was fat. He was half asleep in his sunny garden when Gribble crawled along the road to his house. He was startled when he saw the dragon. He didn't see them very often. He knew that dragons are very rarely ill, which is why he chose to be a dragon doctor. He was rather lazy.

'No fire?' he said when Gribble whispered his problem. 'But all dragons can breathe fire.'

'I can usually,' croaked Gribble, 'but I can't now.'

'Most unusual,' said the dragon doctor. 'Come into the dispensary.'

Gribble followed him into a shop full of asbestos handkerchiefs, tail curlers and other things for dragons to buy as well as many-coloured pills and medicines.

'Thought of the answer,' said the doctor. 'Three dragon pills should do the trick—taken in a glass of paraffin, of course.'

Gribble roared with disappointment and rage. A trail of yellow smoke hung over the dragon scale shampoo and writhed round the claw polish.

'Dragon pills, my claws!' he shouted, and coughed, a vile brown smoke this time.

The doctor was frightened, and crept away to a neighbour's house under cover of the smoke, while Gribble clanked about the garden, getting crosser and crosser, his throat hurting more and more as he roared.

Finally, weeping some great dragon tears he flew into the air again. His head ached and his throat felt as if there was burning fire all the way down to his stomach. But he still could not breathe any fire and he was very hungry.

Chapter 4

He managed to fly back over the Alps, just scraping his tummy on the highest of the mountains. He managed to fly over all of France. He sagged over the Channel, so low that the fish under his shadow dived to the bottom of the sea, thinking it was night and time to sleep. His wings were tired and his throat was so sore he could hardly breathe.

It was nearly supper time. His tummy was rumbling like the inside of the volcano called Etna. His eyes were watering and his nose was hot.

Down below was a wood. Through his watery eyes the green tops looked as if they were wobbling about like soft lime jelly. Gribble felt too ill to think properly. He thought it would be rather soft, a perfect landing place.

If he had landed on the trees, he would have had an even worse tummy ache. Luckily there was a green space right in the middle of the wood and he landed on the grass instead.

He slid for a few yards on his tummy and, though it did not hurt as much as landing on bristly trees would have done, it

was not very comfortable.

So at first, while he lay with his eyes shut, recovering, he didn't see the little house.

When he did open his eyes he thought he must have landed upside-down. The house had smoke coming out of its doors and windows, instead of out of the chimney as it should have done.

A man was running round the outside of the house, opening more doors and windows for the

smoke to come out. Then he ran inside again and brought out something which Gribble recognized.

It was a leg of mutton.

Gribble's mouth watered. He hadn't eaten anything since supper time last night and he was absolutely starving. He crawled closer to the smoking house, nearer to the leg of mutton.

The man, whose name was Smith, came out with a large tablecloth, shook it, so that great

clouds of smoke signalled into
the air, and went inside again.

Gribble crawled closer.

He was just about to breathe
and bite, in his usual way, so that
the outside would be all crisp and
crunchy and the inside pink and

juicy, when Smith startled him
by coming out of a door rather
suddenly.

'Just the fellow I need!' he said. 'My chimney is blocked and the fire's gone out so I can't cook my supper. Just blow on this leg of mutton, there's a good chap.'

'No fire,' said Gribble miserably, but thankful that he had been stopped in time. It would have been dreadful to ruin another leg of mutton with paraffin fumes.

'That's right' said Smith 'It's gone out. I'd be very grateful for your help.'

'No, no,' said Gribble. 'You don't understand. I can't.'

And he puffed to show Smith.

'Oh, not here,' said Smith, alarmed. 'You'll have the woods on fire.'

'No, I won't' said Gribble. 'I can't breathe fire. I don't know what's the matter.'

'You do look rather feverish,' said Smith. 'Come inside while I get rid of the rest of this smoke then we'll have a look at your throat. Just a bit of a cold, I should think.'

Gribble hiccupped miserably on Smith's hall floor and watched the man wave the rest of the smoke outside with his tablecloth. Then he flicked a duster over his table and chairs.

'That's better,' said Smith, when he had finished. 'Open wide.'

He pulled up a chair and stood on it to get a better view of Gribble's great throat. 'H'm. Not so good. I should think a

dragon pill . . .'

Gribble tried to roar, but only
a small sound came out. So did a

great deal of black smoke, which filled Smith's house and darkened his face.

'Pills!' gasped the dragon. 'Had *three*!'

'Funny, that,' said Smith, and opened all the windows again. 'Three pills are usually enough to cure dragon colds.'

He looked sadly at Gribble, who looked sadly back.

'Anybody in?' shouted a voice through one of the open windows.

Chapter 5

He appeared at the door, a man with a face as sooty as Smith's had become. He carried a round brush and a bundle of sticks on his shoulder.

'Ah, the sweep,' said Smith.

'I'm very glad to see you. Just here, man. Come inside while I clean up.'

'What's wrong with old leather wings, then?' asked the sweep, looking at Gribble's miserable face. He rolled a black cloth in front of the fireplace and began to screw lengths of pole on to the brush.

'Sore throat,' said Smith, dusting the sweep's shoes as he went past.

'No fire,' said Gribble and sighed, so that more soot rose into the air and settled on to the tables and chairs.

'No fire?' said the sweep. 'Bad, that, for a dragon. Here, let's have a look.'

Smith pulled up a chair for the sweep to stand on and Gribble opened wide.

'You know what's the matter with you,' said the sweep, and climbed down from the chair. 'You're all bunged up, you are.'

He unscrewed his brush from Smith's chimney and went on, 'You need a sweep, that's what you need. Simple as that.'

Gribble had been all ready to roar if the sweep had said anything about pills, but instead he smiled, an enormous smile that nearly reached his ears.

'Better come outside,' said the sweep. 'Enough smoke in this place as it is.'

'The trees!' Mind the trees!' fussed Smith. 'Face downwind!'

The sweep turned Gribble so that his jaws pointed down Smith's road, well away from the trees.

'Now breathe in a minute while I measure how far to go.'

Gribble obediently breathed in while the sweep took one of the rods and measured the length of the dragon's jaw and his neck.

'Don't want to go too far and have your breakfast up with the soot, do we?' he said.

'Had no breakfast,' choked Gribble as the brush went down his throat.

'What's that?' said the sweep,

and screwed on another rod.

'No break-whOOOOOSH!' said Gribble, and a stream of red-hot cinders splashed out of his mouth and settled on the road in front of him.

A strange thing like a flaming red lollipop on a stick followed and fell with a smack into a puddle, where it sizzled and went out.

'My best brush!' said the sweep. 'I told you to breathe in.'

Gribble tried to look sorry, but he was too pleased.

He breathed, very gently. There it was: a beautiful, hot red flame. No smoke at all.

Finally the sweep cleaned Smith's chimney. It was not done very well, as the sweep's spare brush was not a very good one. But it was clean enough for Smith to lay a fire and for Gribble to breathe gently on the sticks and logs to light it.

Smith put the leg of mutton on the spit to roast and invited the sweep to stay. Gribble lay by the stove, hissing gently, like a kettle on the boil, ready to breathe on the meat if the fire did not cook it properly.

And they all had mutton for supper—crisp and crunchy outside and pink and juicy inside, just the way they liked it.